Dear Kathryn
I miss o

Happy Spring —
love
Mary

Rabén & Sjögren Stockholm

Originally published in Sweden by Rabén & Sjögren
under the title *Kanin-Kalas,*
copyright © 1987 by Lena Anderson
All rights reserved
Library of Congress catalog card number: 88-61822
First edition, 1988
Second printing 1990
Printed in Italy.

ISBN 91 29 59134 1

R & S Books are distributed in the United States of America
by Farrar, Straus and Giroux, New York;
in the United Kingdom by Ragged Bears, Andover;
in Canada by Vanwell Publishing, St.Catharines
and in Australia by ERA Publications, Adelaide

Lena Anderson
BUNNY PARTY

R&S
BOOKS

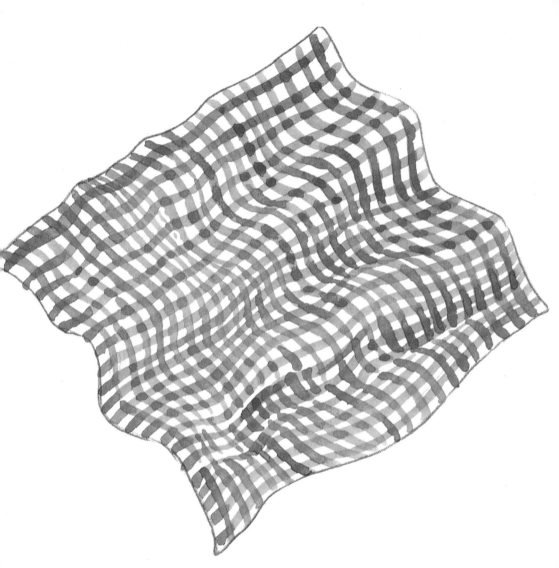

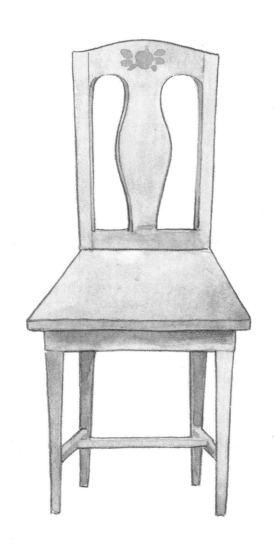